P9-DVO-865

The Fire Station

by Robert Munsch
illustrations by Michael Martchenko

Annick Press Ltd.
Toronto • New York • Vancouver

Eighteenth printing, December 2004

Annick Press Ltd.

We acknowledge the support of the Canada Council for the Arts, the Ontario
Arts Council, and the Government of Canada through the Book Publishing Industry
Development Program (BPIDP) for our publishing activities.

Cataloging in Publication Data

Munsch, Robert N., 1945–
The fire station

(Munsch for kids)
ISBN 1-55037-170-3 (bound) ISBN 1-55037-171-1 (pbk.)

I. Martchenko, Michael. II. Title. III. Series:
Munsch, Robert N., 1945– Munsch for kids.

PS8576.U575 1991 jC813'.54 C90-095561-9
PZ7.M8Fi 1991

Distributed in Canada by: Published in the U.S.A. by Annick Press (U.S.) Ltd.
Firefly Books Ltd.   Distributed in the U.S.A. by:
66 Leek Crescent   Firefly Books (U.S.) Inc.
Richmond Hill, ON   P.O. Box 1338
L4B 1H1   Ellicott Station
                                   Buffalo, NY 14205

Printed and bound in Canada by
Friesens, Altona, Manitoba.

visit us at: **www.annickpress.com**

To Holly Martchenko, Toronto, Ontario
and to Michael Villamore and
Sheila Prescott, Coos Bay, Oregon

Michael and Sheila were walking down the street. As they passed the fire station Sheila said, "Michael! Let's go ride a fire truck."

"Well," said Michael, "I think maybe I should ask my mother, and I think maybe I should ask my father and I think maybe..."

"I think we should go in," said Sheila. Then she grabbed Michael's hand and pulled him up to the door.

Sheila knocked: BLAM – BLAM – BLAM – BLAM – BLAM. A large fireman came out and asked, "What can I do for you?"

"Well," said Michael, "maybe you could show us a fire truck and hoses and rubber boots and ladders and all sorts of stuff like that."

"Certainly," said the fireman.

"And maybe," said Sheila, "you will let us drive a fire truck?"

"Certainly not," said the fireman.

They went in and looked at ladders and hoses and big rubber boots. Then they looked at little fire trucks and big fire trucks and enormous fire trucks. When they were done Michael said, "Let's go."

"Right," said Sheila. "Let's go into the enormous fire truck."

While they were in the truck, the fire alarm went off: CLANG – CLANG – CLANG – CLANG – CLANG.

"Oh, no!" said Michael.

"Oh, yes!" said Sheila. Then she grabbed Michael and pulled him into the back seat.

Firemen came running from all over. They slid down poles and ran down stairs. Then they jumped onto the truck and drove off. The firemen didn't look in the back seat. Michael and Sheila were in the back seat.

They came to an enormous fire. Lots of yucky-coloured smoke got all over everything. It coloured Michael yellow, green and blue. It coloured Sheila purple, green and yellow.

When the fire chief saw them he said, "What are you doing here!"

Sheila said, "We came in the fire truck. We thought maybe it was a bus. We thought maybe it was a taxi. We thought maybe it was an elevator. We thought maybe..."

"I think maybe I'd better take you home," said the fire chief. He put Michael and Sheila in his car and drove them away.

When Michael got home he knocked on the door. His mother opened it and said, "You messy boy! You can't come in and play with Michael! You're too dirty." She slammed the door right in Michael's face.

"My own mother," said Michael. "She didn't even know me." He knocked on the door again.

His mother opened the door and said, "You dirty boy! You can't come in and play with Michael. You're too dirty. You're absolutely filthy. You're a total mess. You're...Oh, my!...Oh, no!...YOU'RE MICHAEL!"

Michael went inside and lived in the bathtub for three days until he got clean.

When Sheila came home she knocked on the door. Her father opened it and saw an incredibly messy girl. He said, "You can't come in to play with Sheila. You're too dirty." He slammed the door right in her face.

"Ow," said Sheila. "My own father and he didn't even know me."

She kicked and pounded on the door as loudly as she could. Her father opened the door and said, "Now stop that racket, you dirty girl. You can't come in to play with Sheila. You're too dirty. You're absolutely filthy. You're a total mess. You're...Oh, my!...Oh, no!... YOU'RE SHEILA!"

"Right," said Sheila, "I went to a fire in the back of a fire truck and I got all smoky. I WASN'T EVEN SCARED."

Sheila went inside and lived in the bathtub for five days until she got clean.

Then Michael took Sheila on a walk past the police station. He told her, "If you ever take me in another fire truck, I am going to ask the police to put you in jail."

"JAIL!" yelled Sheila. "Let's go look at the jail! What a great idea!"

"Oh, no!" yelled Michael, and Sheila grabbed his hand and pulled him into the police station.